STONE ARCH BOOKS
a capstone imprint

Sports Illustrated KIDS

Don't Wobble on the Wakeboard!

by Chris Kreie
illustrated by Jorge Santillan

STONE ARCH BOOKS
a capstone imprint

Sports Illustrated KIDS *Don't Wobble on the Wakeboard*
is published by Stone Arch Books — A Capstone Imprint
151 Good Counsel Drive, P.O. Box 669
Mankato, Minnesota 56002
www.capstonepub.com

Art Director: Bob Lentz
Graphic Designer: Hilary Wacholz
Production Specialist: Michelle Biedscheid

Timeline photo credits: Shutterstock/bbbb (top right), Ivan
Miladinovic (bottom right), Kris Butler (top left), RTimages
(middle left); Sports Illustrated/Robert Beck (bottom left).

Printed in the United States of America in Stevens Point, Wisconsin.
032011   006111WZF11

Library of Congress Cataloging-in-Publication Data
Kreie, Chris. Don't wobble on the wakeboard! / by Chris Kreie; illustrated by
Jorge H. Santillan.
   p. cm. — (Sports Illustrated kids. Victory School superstars)
Summary: Josh uses all his talent and skills to do the best he can in a camp
wakeboarding competition.
ISBN 978-1-4342-2235-0 (library binding)
ISBN 978-1-4342-3396-7 (pbk.)
   1. Wakeboarding—Juvenile fiction. 2. Competition (Psychology)—Juvenile
fiction. 3. Teamwork (Sports)—Juvenile fiction. [1. Wakeboarding—Fiction.
2. Competition (Psychology)—Fiction. 3. Teamwork (Sports)—Fiction.] I.
Santillan, Jorge, ill. II. Title. III. Title: Do not wobble on the wakeboard! IV.
Series: Sports Illustrated kids. Victory School superstars.
PZ7.K8793Do 2011
[Fic]—dc22   2011002311

TABLE of CONTENTS

JOSH CHAMPS

Wakeboarding

AGE: 10
GRADE: 4
SUPER SPORTS ABILITY: Super Skating

Playa Victoria Superstars:

 JOSH

 CARMEN   TYLER

PLAYA VICTORIA

Don't let Playa Victoria's relaxed vibe fool you. Here, athletes
work hard as they soak up the rays. The best of the best train
at this gorgeous beach resort. Learn summer sports like beach
volleyball, wakeboarding, and surfing from the top experts.

1. Surf Shack
2. Volleyball Court
3. Main Boat Dock
4. Resort Lodge
5. Bungalows

"Wake up, Josh. It's time to get out of bed." I open my eyes. Brendan, my roommate from Victory Sports School, is standing over me.

"What time is it?" I ask.

"It's almost eight," says Brendan. "We're going to be late. Everyone else already headed outside."

I look around at our bungalow. I cannot believe we get to spend our vacation in this awesome cottage on a California beach.

When I open the front door, the sweet smell of the Pacific Ocean blows in. I take a deep breath and jog toward the rest of the group. Students from Victory are lined up at the beach next to students from another sports school.

"Nice of you to join us," says Kenzie. She's a friend of mine from Victory.

"I could have slept all day," I say.

"Okay, students," says a tall man with blond hair and a dark tan. He is one of several adults standing in front of us.

"My name is Anthony," he says, "and we will be your sports instructors here at Playa Victoria Resort. As you all know, there will be a tournament at the end of the week. Students from Victory School and students from Champions School will compete for the Playa Victoria Cup."

"Yeah! Go Victory!" I shout.

"I like the enthusiasm," Anthony says, grinning. "The sports you will be competing in are beach volleyball, surfing, windsurfing, kayaking, and wakeboarding."

"This is great," says Kenzie. "I've gotten really good at volleyball."

"And I kayak on the river with my dad all the time," says Brendan.

"There is one catch," says Anthony. "You must compete in a sport you have never tried before."

"No way," I say. The athletes from both schools groan.

"Good luck to all of you," says Anthony.

All of us Superstars meet to decide who will compete in each sport. Brendan chooses surfing.

Kenzie and I know nothing about wakeboarding. But it sounds fun, so we decide to give it a try.

Out on the
Water

Later that day, Kenzie and I are on a boat skimming across the ocean. Anthony is driving. Sitting across from us are two students from Champions School.

"My name is Josh," I say. "And this is Kenzie."

"I'm Hannah," says the girl.

"And I'm John," says the boy.

Anthony shuts off the boat's engine. "Okay," he says. "Who's first?"

"I'll go!" says Kenzie. She jumps over the side of the boat. With her life jacket on, she bobs in the waves.

"Keep your knees bent and your arms straight to start," says Anthony. "Don't try anything fancy your first time, okay?"

"Got it," says Kenzie, smiling.

Kenzie has a hard time getting up on her board. When she finally gets up, she lasts only a few seconds before crashing back to the water.

Next up is John. He doesn't do much better than Kenzie. He keeps falling over.

Finally it's my turn. "Hit it!" I yell. Anthony guns the boat forward.

I'm up immediately. It's easy. I think my super skating skills helps me feel comfortable on the board.

The boat pulls me over the water. I'm relaxed so I decide to try something fun. I shift my weight to the right and dig the edge of the board into the water.

Then I quickly shift my weight to the left and dig the other edge of the board into the water. I fly across the waves.

I hit the wake of water created by the boat. I bend my knees and jump into the air. My landing isn't perfect but I don't fall down. I tell myself, "Don't wobble on the wakeboard!"

I do a few more jumps before I'm done.

"You looked great out there!" says Kenzie.

"I felt great," I say.

Hannah is last to go. She bounces over a few waves, and then flies off to the left of the boat's wake. She looks graceful on her board.

Hannah pulls the rope tight, and then suddenly rips herself across the wake. *Whoosh!* Her jump is much higher than mine.

She lands easily, and then takes off in the other direction. Again she hits the wake, but this time her jump is twice as high as her first one. Kenzie's mouth drops open.

Finally Hannah pauses. She pulls herself as far to the right as she can before blasting across the wake one final time. Kenzie and I watch in shock as Hannah pulls her body backward and does a complete flip before landing back on the water.

"Whoo-whee!" she screams.

"Wow, she's awesome!" Kenzie says.

I'm speechless.

CHAPTER 3

A Liar?

We're all hanging out on the beach after practice. After all those falls, lying in the warm sand feels awesome.

"Hannah," says Anthony. "You were really good out there."

"Maybe too good," I say.

"What's that supposed to mean?" Hannah says.

"It means we don't believe this is your first time on a wakeboard," says Kenzie.

"Oh, really?" says Hannah.

John leans forward. "Are you calling her a liar?" he asks.

"Maybe athletes from Victory lie," says Hannah. "But at Champions School, we have more honor than that."

"Okay, guys," says Anthony. "Break it up."

"Do you want to know why wakeboarding is so easy for me?" asks Hannah.

"Yeah," says Kenzie. "We do."

"It's because Hannah is a champion snowboarder," John says. "You should see her rip the halfpipe."

"That makes sense," says Anthony. "Some of the best wakeboarders I have ever trained are the ones who spend their winters on a snowboard."

"Snowboarding, huh?" I ask. I still feel a little suspicious, but if Anthony says it makes sense, maybe it does.

"That's right," says Hannah with a glare.

I look at Kenzie. She nods.

"Okay, we believe you," I say.

"Yeah," says Kenzie. "Sorry we called you a liar."

"You shouldn't be so quick to judge people, but no hard feelings," says Hannah. We all shake hands. "Good luck this week."

"We're going to need more than luck," I say. "I better learn how to do a flip. And I better learn how to do it fast." We all smile.

CHAPTER

4

Tournament
Day

Kenzie and I have practiced tons over the past three days. Kenzie has improved a lot. Her spins are really tight.

My jumps have gotten higher, but I'm bummed out. I haven't been able to land even one flip. But I can't waste time thinking about that today. It's finally Friday — tournament day.

All the competitors are lined up on the beach.

Anthony explains the rules. "In each event, teams can score up to ten points for their school," he says. "Let the Playa Victoria Tournament begin!"

Athletes from both schools let out a loud shout.

Kenzie, Josh, and I cheer for our Victory teammates. They lose the volleyball match, but they win the kayaking competition.

The tournament is tied 10 to 10. I yell, "Let's go Victory!"

"In the next three events, teams will score ten points for winning the event," explains Anthony. "Or five points for performing well."

Our Victory teammates fly high over the waves in the windsurfing competition. They land the most amazing spins and jumps.

"Wow!" says Kenzie. She nudges me with her elbow. "Did you see that?"

"I'm watching the same thing you're watching," I say. We both laugh.

Victory School takes ten points in the windsurfing event. The Champions team does well and scores five. The score is 20 points for Victory and 15 for Champions.

"I'm up," says Brendan. The surfing event is next. "Wish me luck."

We watch Brendan ride the waves. "He's amazing!" says Kenzie. "It's hard to believe he just learned this week."

"Hang ten, dude!" I shout.

"What does that mean?" asks Kenzie.

"I have no idea," I say, laughing. "It's what surfers say."

Brendan and his teammate dominate the surfing event and win ten points. Again, the athletes from Champions score five points.

"It's our turn," says Kenzie.

"Let's do this thing," I say. We share a high five.

CHAPTER 5

Why Risk the Flip?

"With one event left in the tournament," says Anthony, "the score is Victory School: 30, and Champions School: 20."

"Do you know what this means?" asks Kenzie. "Even if Hannah and John score ten points, all we have to do is score five points to win the tournament."

John goes first. His performance is clean, but it has very little style or flash.

Kenzie is next. She does ten different spins and never crashes once. She has gotten so good!

"Great job," I say to her when she gets back in the boat.

"Thanks!" she says with a huge grin.

Hannah is up on her board and immediately lands three huge jumps.

After a few spins she pulls out wide to prepare for her flip. She flies toward the wake and launches herself into the air. But the flip is short. She falls hard on the water.

Kenzie pulls me aside. "Now you don't have to do your flip," she says. "If you do a clean, simple run we'll score five points for sure."

"I need to do the flip," I say.

"We don't need ten points," Kenzie says. "Why risk it?"

"I need to try my hardest and do my best," I say. "That's what we do at Victory. We challenge ourselves to be the best athletes we can possibly be. We don't go halfway."

I jump into the water. Anthony blasts the boat forward, and I am up on my board.

I do some easy spins first before pulling myself off to the right. I fly over the wake and land a solid jump. Kenzie gives me a thumbs-up from the boat.

I do two more jumps before preparing myself for the flip. I go wide to the left. I'm ready.

I pull the rope tight, and then I dig my board into the water. I skim across the ocean and hit the wake. I'm flying.

I quickly flex my body backward and pull the board into the air. I hold onto the rope with just one hand. I'm upside down over the water.

Finally, I bend my knees and reach my board toward the water. I slam against the waves. My knees buckle. *Don't wobble on the wakeboard*, I think.

I get my balance, then stand straight up on the board. I land it! My first flip!

Back on the beach, Anthony announces the final score. "In the wakeboarding competition, scoring five points is the team from Champions School. Winning the event and scoring ten points is the team from Victory!"

"We did it!" Kenzie yells, grabbing me into a big hug.

"Way to go, guys!" shouts Brendan.

"With that win, the Playa Victoria Cup goes to Victory School!" shouts Anthony.

We all rush up to receive our trophy. All around me, there are Superstars hugging and high-fiving each other.

"We won the tournament!" I shout.

Hannah and John congratulate us. "Great win," says Hannah.

"We couldn't have done it if you hadn't pushed us to be our best this week," I say.

"I tell you what," says Hannah. "Come to Champions School some time, and I'll teach you guys how to carve it up on a snowboard."

Kenzie, Brendan, and I look at each other. We all smile. "Deal!" we say.

GLOSSARY

bungalow (BUHNG-guh-loh)—a small house

competitors (kuhm-PET-i-turs)—people who take part in a contest and try to win

congratulate (kuhn-GRACH-uh-late)—to tell someone that he or she has done a good job

dominate (DOM-uh-nate)—to control or rule

enthusiasm (en-THOO-zee-az-um)—great excitement or interest

immediately (i-MEE-dee-it-lee)—now or at once

performance (pur-FOR-muhnss)—the doing of an action

suspicious (suh-SPISH-uhss)—if you feel suspicious, you think that something is wrong or bad

tournament (TUR-nuh-muhnt)—a series of contests in which many teams try to win a championship

ABOUT THE AUTHOR

CHRIS KREIE

Chris Kreie lives in Minnesota with his wife and two children. He works as a school librarian and writes books in his free time. Some of his other books include *There Are No Figure Eights in Hockey* and *Who Wants to Play Just for Kicks?* from the Victory School Superstars series and *The Curse of Raven Lake* and *Wild Hike*.

ABOUT THE ILLUSTRATOR

JORGE SANTILLAN

Jorge Santillan got his start illustrating in the children's sections of local newspapers. He opened his own illustration studio in 2005. His creative team specializes in books, comics, and children's magazines. Jorge lives in Mendoza, Argentina, with his wife, Bety; son, Luca; and their four dogs, Fito, Caro, Angie, and Sammy.

WAKEBOARDING IN HISTORY

1946 The **International Waterski Federation** is formed. It is renamed the International Waterski and Wakeboard Federation in 2009. This group is in charge of developing rules for the sport.

1980s People begin **surfing** while being pulled behind a boat.

1985 Tony Finn, a surfer, creates the skurfer. It is an early version of the wakeboard, combining features of a water ski and a surfboard.

1990 The first skurfer **championship** is televised.

1992 The first professional wakeboarding events are held in the United States.

1993 Wakeboarding gets its first magazine: *Wake Boarding*.

1996 Wakeboarding is an event at the **X Games** for the first time.

1999 Wakeboarding is included in the first Gravity Games.

2000 Obstacles like sliders and **ramps** are added to the wakeboarding course.

2011 TransWorld Business announces they will cover wakeboarding in a magazine and on its web site.

Josh Champs Lives Up to His Name!

If you liked reading Josh's wakeboard adventure, check out his other sports stories.

There Are No Figure Eights in Hockey

Josh is already a figure skating champion, so he is looking for a new challenge. Hockey seems perfect for his super skating. But out on the ice, Josh realizes this new sport won't be so easy. After all, there are no figure eights in hockey.

Who Wants to Play Just for Kicks?

Over spring break, Josh's friends want to take time off from their sports and play soccer just for fun. Josh would rather practice hockey, but he gives the game a try. When he doesn't catch on, he wonders, "Who wants to play just for kicks?"

STONE ARCH BOOKS
a capstone imprint